WHEN CATS GO WRONG

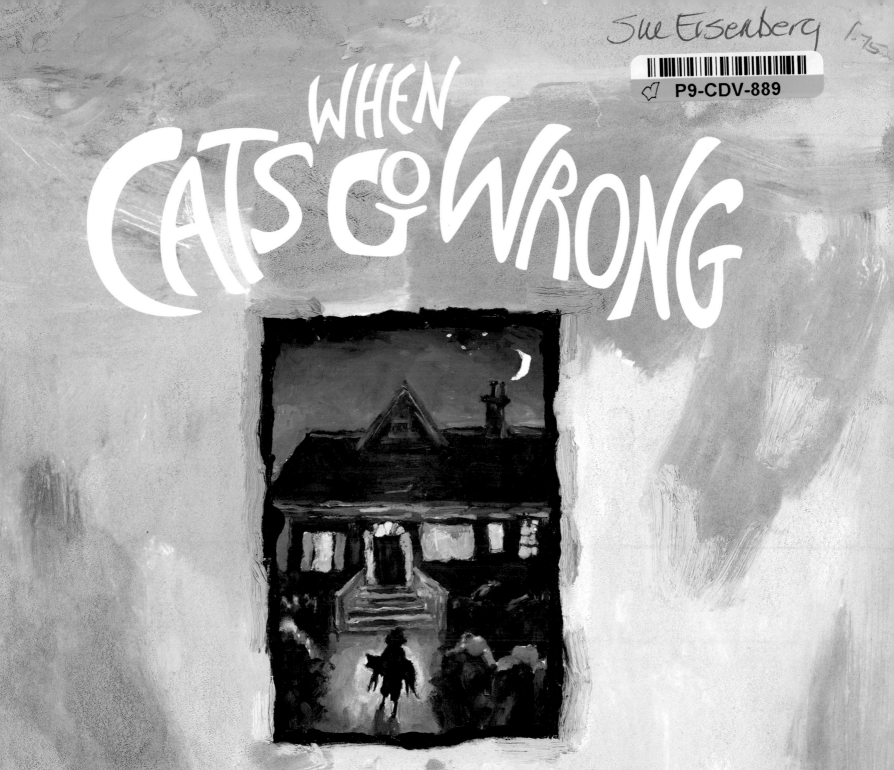

Written and performed by **Norm Hacking**   Illustrations by **Cynthia Nugent**

RAINCOAST BOOKS

Vancouver

To my wonderful mother Kathy O. and to my family, Ella, John and John Karach Jr.,

who early on instilled in me a lifelong love for cats … even the naughty kind.

Thanks to Fred Becker, Shirley Gibson, Kirk Elliott, Maddy and Red,

and of course, the wonderful Cynthia Nugent. — NH

For my dear friend Norma Larson. — CN

Words and music copyright © 2006 by Norm Hacking • Illustrations copyright © 2006 by Cynthia Nugent

First paperback edition

Raincoast Books gratefully acknowledges the ongoing support of the Canada Council for the Arts, the British Columbia Arts Council and the Government of Canada through the Book Publishing Industry Development Program (BPIDP).

Edited by Simone Doust
Cover and interior design by Elisa Gutiérez

LIBRARY AND ARCHIVES CANADA CATALOGUING IN PUBLICATION
Hacking, Norm, 1950–
    When cats go wrong / Norm Hacking; illustrated by Cynthia Nugent. —1st paperback ed.

ISBN 10: 1-55192-917-1
ISBN 13: 978-1-55192-917-0

    1. Cats—Juvenile fiction. 2. Tango (Dance)—History—Juvenile literature.
I. Nugent, Cynthia, 1954– II. Title.
PS8615.A35W44 2006   jC813'.6   C2005-905749-1

LIBRARY OF CONGRESS CATALOGUE NUMBER: 2005904836

Raincoast Books
9050 Shaughnessy Street
Vancouver, British Columbia
Canada   V6P 6E5
www.raincoast.com

In the United States:
Publishers Group West
1700 Fourth Street
Berkeley, California
94710

Printed in China.
10 9 8 7 6 5 4 3 2 1

Sometimes when I leave the house

I must admit I worry

I try to do what I must do
And get back in a hurry.

The thought of what a cat might do
When left at home alone

Makes me fear what I might find
When I come back home.

Wasn't there a goldfish
In the goldfish bowl?

Wasn't Mother's knitting basket
Full of balls of wool?

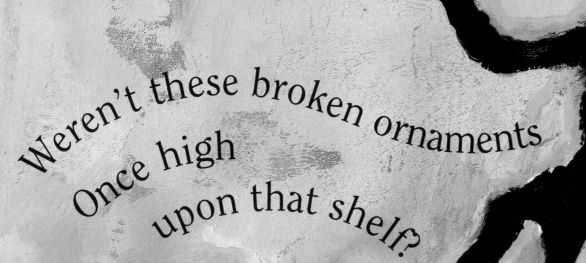

Weren't these broken ornaments
Once high
upon that shelf?

Forgive me for I guess I'm feeling sorry for myself.

Life with a naughty kitty

Isn't very pretty.

So I sing this mournful song

About when cats go wrong.

The couch is ripped and torn apart,
The stuffing is pulled out.
The litter box is empty
With the gravel strewn about.

Everything's in disarray,
It makes me grump and mutter.
There's cat hair
on the tablecloth
And tongue marks on the butter.

Life with a naughty kitty

Isn't very pretty.

So I sing this mournful song

About when cats go wrong.

Budgie's looking traumatized
With feathers on the floor,
Lucky thing a pussy cat
Can't fit through the cage door.

There're claw marks on the lampshades
And paw prints on the mirror.
The missing shoelace mystery
Is now becoming clearer.

It's just another cat toy
To amuse my little pet,
Like the nice lace curtains
That are so much fun to shred,

Like the ball of twine
That's been unravelled from its spool,
Like the worn-out cat-nip mouse

Covered in cat drool.

Life with a naughty kitty

Isn't very pretty.

So I sing this mournful song

About when cats go wrong.

♫♪♪ What's in a Tune ♫♪♪

The song "When Cats Go Wrong" is especially funny because it is composed in a form of serious, passionate music called "tango". The tango is also a kind of dance done with a partner. When you use a serious art form like opera or tango to describe a funny subject, it's called High Burlesque. Norm Hacking's deep serious voice when he sings funny lines like "tongue marks on the butter" is a perfect example.

The most prominent musical instrument in the tango orchestra is the bandoneon, a kind of accordian. In When Cats Go Wrong, the boy plays the bandoneon while he sings his mournful song.

Both the music and dance of the tango started in Argentina in the early 1900s. Its popularity quickly spread around the world. In Paris tangomania influenced food, fashion and social life. Yellow was even declared the official tango colour.

At that time, Paris was bubbling with artistic activity of all kinds including art, music and theatre. The poster art advertising these activities was done in a bright and bold style. They featured a lot of orange and yellow, and had interesting flowing shapes and rhythmic lines. Even the lettering had a musical look. You could say that the posters looked like a tango sounds. The most famous artist who made these posters was Toulouse Lautrec. The art in this book was inspired by both the tango itself, and the celebrated posters of Paris.